AF429525

Princess Jasmine and Her Lovely Pet

By

Rarsa Amlas

<u>**Disclaimer :**</u>

This Book Contains Sexual Contents (18+)

Princess Jasmine and Her Lovely Pet.

"Mmmm..." Princess Jasmine slowly let out, with a sigh of desire, as she continued to pleasure herself.

She lay on her back, surrounded by her lavish, royal bed adorned with fine, silk purple fittings, stuffed with the softest goose feathers money could buy. The the long, sea-green curtains surrounding her bed were drawn closed, though she was alone in the palace tonight, she enjoyed the solitude whenever she lay down to masturbate.

Jasmine had removed off all her clothes and threw

them aside the bed, she lay completely stripped and naked. She quietly let out another small moan, and softly arched her back as she continued to finger herself, her hot, slick pussy creating small jolts of immense pleasure as she rubbed her clitoris, and moved her index and middle finger rhythmically in and out of herself. Her hips automatically moving back in forth with the motion.

With her free hand, she caressed her small, erect nipples. She's always enjoyed gently pinching them whenever she fucked herself. She alternated between squeezing and fondling her left breast and working her aroused nipple as her fingers slid in and out of her.

"Oohh…" she sighed, slightly louder. No one was in the palace, no one usually was ever around except for her tiger Rajah. She frequently would forget she needn't be quiet when she masturbated, yet was sometimes shy in making noise.

Her breaths became shorter and briefer as the pleasure built inside of her. Her pussy extensively growing wetter and slicker. Her two fingers moving in and out, ravishing her body with delight.

"...Aah!" she meekly exclaimed as her index finger suddenly struck her g-spot, causing her body to tense and her back to arch further with a wave of pleasure.

She withdrew her dampened fingers and began to run them over her clit. Jasmine threw her head back and ran her free hand's finger through her hair, and grabbed a lock, pulling it softly.

"Oh..Oh, god" she moaned as her fingers circled around her tight pussy faster and faster… Her body tensed even tighter, and she pulled her hair slightly harder as she began to approach her climax.

"Aaaah!" she yelled out, having no qualms about being quiet, "Oh god yes!". Even just making noise fucking herself turned her on much further. She could hear the sound of her hand running over slick pussy and clit even over her short, panting breaths.

Princess Jasmine let out deep moans with every breath, her pussy absolutely drenched with her sexual juices. She felt the pins and needles up and down her legs and spine, her tits softly bouncing back and forth with the rhythm of her fucking herself.

"Oooh, Godddddddd…!" she screamed, "F-Fuck! Oh.. my God!". She rubbed faster and faster around her clit, working it back and forth… it felt amazing, she was so close…she went faster and faster, rubbing harder and harder until suddenly her hot pussy erupted with a flood of sexual pleasure as she brought herself to climax.. She let out a loud moan as her womanhood tightened, and her body shook with delight as she finally cum. Her pussy quivered with her, as her orgasm ravished her body. She panted like an animal in heat as she move her fingers back down inside of her, and furiously slid them in and out – fucking her tight pussy as deep as she could reach. She moaned harder and faster as her juices ran down her sexy, toned legs and onto the sheets, and continued fingering herself as she came, making her orgasm as long and satisfying as she possibly could.

Her fingers traveled around her pussy slower and slower as she inhaled deeply in and out attempting to catch her breath. She slowly ran her slick fingers up her body and to her mouth, circling her tongue around them and licking her sweet pussy juices off. She let out another soft moan and licked her middle and ring fingers, running her tongue around them… she loved the taste. Though she'd already cum, the sexual pleasure still traveled up and down her body…

She was still turned on by tasting her own pussy...She wanted more, she couldn't satisfy her desire by herself anymore... she burned to fucked by something hot, and real. Her mind was filled with fantasies of being fucked senseless by someone, their big cock sliding in and out of her tight pussy...

anyone... she didn't care,
she just wanted it so,
very badly.

She took her fingers out
of her mouth and lay
back, relaxed and spread
out on her bed.

Her womanhood still
burned with desire...
cumming like that was so

unexciting for her
nowadays.

Princess Jasmine
couldn't believe herself
thinking like this...
She'd always been so shy
about sex. She'd never
had a sexual parter
before, she'd never even
seen a man's erect
cock...her father never
allowed men in the

palace... Even if he did, Jasmine hadn't any friends to bring up to her bed who's body's she could explore.

She'd changed so much... just a year prior, at 16, she was even embarrassed to herself masturbating... she'd do it quietly and quickly – lights off, under the covers, with her hand simply slipped down into her nightgown, and would rub herself through her panties...she'd rarely ever penetrate herself. She almost felt ashamed when she put her fingers inside of her.

Perhaps, Jasmine began to think, she just didn't

know how to properly enjoy it. When she first learned how, and started masturbating, she never even considered letting out screams or moans like she just did… she'd never lay back completely naked on her bed with the lights on so she could watch her hand sliding in and out. She'd never pull her hair or pinch her nipples as she fucked herself… and she'd certainly never even consider tasting her own fingers when she'd finished.

Jasmine began to think of how it all changed though… Every time she got more into it – the harder she panted, the louder she was, the harder she fucked herself – the harder she would cum. Now Princess Jasmine loved everything about masturbating.. she'd try almost any new or creative way she could think of to get herself off.

She became wrapped up in her sexual desire… she lived in a palace with people rarely present. All

Jasmine had to do all day was either gaze out at Agrabah through her windows, play with her tiger... or masturbate. She chose the latter quite frequently... sometimes even as much as six or seven times in a day. Her desire was never truly quenched.

The Princess let out a
sigh of discontent.
Though she'd cum just
moments ago, she
realized how unsatisfying
it really was... she
wanted something more.

Princess Jasmine sat
herself up, and moved to
the edge of her bed,
opening her curtains and
hanging her legs off the

side. She rested her elbows on her knees and her chin on her hands and began to think – her perfect, naked body shimmering in the light.

"Now what have I already tried..." she said aloud as she recalled the different methods she'd explored in reaching orgasm.

She'd tried using larger things – fucking herself with fruits, cylinder-shaped pieces of palace decorations, etc. She'd tried different positions while masturbating, fantasizing, masturbating in the bath room with the water pressure nozzles, even occasionally spying on

some of the guards
changing, hoping to see
something exciting –
she'd tried everything
she could think of. She
wanted something better..
she had no care weather
it was normal or "kinky".
Everything eventually
became dull and boring.
Her entire life was dull
and boring, she never
had anything to do alone

in the palace… Honestly, she just wanted to be fucked, and hard.

She threw herself back in annoyance onto her bed with a dissatisfied grunt of "Hmph!". She lay comfortably, her legs bent and spread wide open and her hands behind her head and tousled hair. It almost looked like an invitation for the next person that comes in the door to fuck her – she chuckled, she actually wished that would happen.

At that moment...the door to her bedroom creaked open slightly, Jasmine's heart spiked with both fear and excitement... she was completely naked and sprawled out upon her bed, her pussy still wet from her masturbation, what would they think if someone saw her like this?

"Oh...it's just you" Jasmine said with some disappointment as her dearest friend, her pet tiger Rajah, walked in the door.

Rajah's ears went back and he hung his head low at Jasmine's unenthusiastic greeting of him.

"Haha, I'm sorry Rajah I didn't mean it like that," she explained as she propped her upper body up upon her elbows,

"I was just kind of hoping you'd be someone else..."

"...but I can't fuck a tiger now can I?" she finished with a giggle.

The large serbian tiger tilted his head in confusion as it began walking over to

Jasmine's bed. Though she knew the tiger didn't truly understand her speech, she would always talk to him… He was amazingly intelligent, she would swear that Rajah would always understand what she meant, even if he didn't understand fully what she said. She could tell him anything.

The tiger walked up and sat on the floor in front of Jasmine's sprawled out body at the foot of her bed. Again, he tilted his head inquisitively as he examined her.

"What's the matter, boy?" she asked trying

to decipher his strange looks.

"You feeling okay? Hungy? ...or... Umm," she began to ask.

"...Oh!" she suddenly realized, blushing slightly, "you've never really seen your master naked before, have you?"

Rajah's eyes studied Jasmine's unusual appearance, and his head tilted from one side to the other.

Jasmine sat up onto her knees, resting her ass upon her heels. She moved her right hand down over her crotch to cover her still slick, hairless vagina, and positioned her left forearm across her chest and covered her breasts.

"There we go, all better" she said with a smile, "C'mere boy"

Rajah perked up immediately and leapt upon the bed next to his master, licking her face with great enthusiasm.

"Hahaha," Jasmine laughed in reaction, "stop it Rajah, haha, it tickles!". She let her perfect, young breasts fall back down as she removed her left arm from holding them to move the overly-affectionate tiger from licking her face off.

She gave the tiger a hug, and scuffed the fur around his neck and face. Rajah popped up and lay half his body across Jasmine's lap as he enjoyed his praise. Jasmine kissed the tiger on the nose, and lay back down onto her bed, her right hand still covering her moist womanhood. She didn't care if the tiger saw her naked… but her naked was an unusual appearance to Rajah, and didn't want to confuse him as she's rarely this exposed to her tiger.

Rajah sleepily lay across Jasmine's torso, his chin resting atop Jasmine's left breast. She continued to stroke his fur with her left hand… with her right hand, she casually slipped a finger inside of her pussy, and squeezing her womanhood with her other fingers.

Jasmine sighed.

"Urgh… Life is boring, Rajah…" she said lazily, as the tiger continued to lay still. "I'm just so sick of this," she continued, "nothing to do in this place, I don't see anyone hardly ever, and…getting myself off takes forever now.. and it usually sucks too."

She let out a final sigh as she closed her eyes... quickly enough she drifted off into sleep.

She was exhausted... masturbating for as long as she did took a tole on her energy levels. She didn't worry though, she hadn't anything to do today and there wasn't a soul to bother her in the entire palace.

"hmm..?" Jasmine stirred, as she softly awoke from her slumber. It was even darker outside... She could barely see even with candles lit inside her room. It must've been quite late, she reasoned.

Her sleepy, slightly delirious brain felt something strange.. Something ..moving around slowly down below.

"Rajah?" she asked softly

Jasmine raised an inquisitive eyebrow, and raised herself up. She reached to open her bed curtains to let some light from the lit candles in her room illuminate the situation.

Her eyes focused, it was indeed Rajah.

"Haha, you silly tiger..." she joked, "what on earth are you doing mister?"

Rajah was 'investigating'. He was positioned between Jasmine's legs with his head between her thighs. He poked around up and down her legs with his nose, and occasionally lick parts of her thighs. He'd never seen Jasmine naked like this.. never seen his master's tight, young pussy. Though he didn't know exactly what he was doing or looking at, Jasmine's vagina was a curious sight to him.

"I'm still the same Jasmine I promise, Rajah" she softly joked, "just without clothes, goofy cat.". She saw no harm in her tiger being curious, and no sleepy motivation to force the large cat to move.

Rajah didn't understand. He continued to work his way up her legs and inner thighs... and eventually made his way up to her hot, moist core.

Jasmine gasped, and immediately sat up in reaction.

"Woah, boy, that's off limits to you" she said, reaching down, about to move her tiger's head from getting too close to her womanhood.

"You're not allowed there-" she began, but was suddenly cut off as Rajah decided to give Jasmine's pussy a small experimental lick with his large, smooth tongue.

Rajah's warm huge tongue slipped all the way up from the bottom Jasmine's pussy, and directly over her clitoris... She let out a small involuntary moan in pleasure. It felt... so unusual. Unusual, but good. Jasmine laughed at the situation, if only Rajah knew just what he was up to.

"Raja... No, what are you doing..." she said with a laugh, as she began to realize what was happening, and attempted to ignore the wave of pleasure that the tiger just sent through her body. She placed her hands on his head to move him away.

The tiger, misreading Jasmine's tone, reasoned Jasmine wanted him to do it again.

Rajah gave her pussy another soft lick.. this time, extending his large tongue out further and licking slower. The taste was warm and sweet to Rajah, the tiger enjoyed it immensely.

"Oh my GOD" she whispered as her eyes

fluttered closed in pleasure... The huge tiger tongue was unlike anything she'd felt before.. Jasmine felt chills up and down her body... her pussy was dripping wet in seconds.

"Rajah... no you...can't..." she opposed... She couldn't let her tiger do this to her, could she? No... It's just not natural...

Her hands were still on his head, but she hadn't the ability to make him move.. she couldn't even think straight after that last lick.

Rajah continued, and started licking Jasmine's

increasingly wet pussy like he would lick his paws after a meal. His tongue worked up her pussy quicker and harder with each pass.

Jasmine put her hand on her face… she began to pant deeply… "Rajahh…Oh…f-fuck…that's…"

The tiger's massive tongue licked every inch of Jasmine's hot womanhood on each taste. His tong was so big, and powerful, it would travel slightly inside of her before it made its way over her clitoris.

The feeling of being penetrated by the hot, moist tiger tongue as well as the spikes of lust that shook her body when her clit was touched overwhelmed Jasmine. Her back arched deeply, and her beautiful breasts bounced in the air as Rajah ate her pussy. Her crotch involuntarily thrusted in motion with Rajah's licking.

She'd never felt this feeling before, she was absolutely soaked... She didn't know what to do, her tiger was giving her this unbelievable pleasure... but he was an animal, it just wasn't right.

Her panting sped up and up... She let out a soft scream in desire.

"Oh.. my GOD, Rajah... Oh fuckk... I'm so clos-" She began to scream, out of breath.

No, she couldn't let his happen.. she couldn't let

her tiger make her cum like this.

Jasmine summon all her will power… and hopped up, away from Rajah's majestic tongue, and covered her absolutely drenched pussy with her hand. She was so fucking close.. even just touching herself to cover up almost made her cum.

But she couldn't let this happen. Rajah was her pet.

"Rajah.. No, bad boy…" she attempted to scold, but was almost completely out of breath.

Rajah gave Jasmine a confused look.

Jasmine wanted with every part of her to grab his head and have him finish her off. She'd never been this turned on in her life. Her whole body was shaking, her juices were running down her fingers as she tried to cover herself up. It was unreal.

She quickly got up from her bed, and began to walk towards the door. If she stayed there temptation would overwhelm her, she wanted it too badly to trust herself. But getting your pussy licked by your pet, it was just so unnatural and immoral to Jasmine, there's no way she could ever let that happen again. She wouldn't be able to control herself.

Jasmine could barely walk straight, she nearly couldn't feel her legs from Rajah's tongue.

She made her way out of her bed chamber and out into the lavish royal hallway, walking through the palace naked and soaking wet. She headed for the bath-chamber, she just needed to clear her mind.

Jasmine eventually made it to the bath area – A huge chamber of brilliant white marble, and a massive circular marble bath tub in the center – and began to run the warm water. As the tub slowly filled, she sat upon the edge with her feet in the water, replaying the events that just passed in her head.

She was still unbelievably aroused… She needed to finish herself off now… but it wouldn't be the same.

How on earth could she make herself cum with just her hands after the feeling she just had of having her pussy eaten out by such a huge, strong tongue.

Rajah quickly trotted into the bath-chamber to find out why his master had suddenly ran off. Her eyes were closed as she recalled what just happened – her hand traveling around her pussy, her fingers going in and out... It wasn't doing anything for her. She was so close, but couldn't cum like this. She was going crazy, she couldn't think straight.

Her eyes cracked open, and she saw her tiger

sitting there, patiently watching her masturbate. He gave a saddened-confused look.

Jasmine sighed.

"I'm sorry Rajah," she began, "It's not that it didn't feel good... actually it felt great...

but I just can't let you do that..."

Rajah yawned, and remained sitting with his depressed demeanor. He wondered if he had upset his master somehow?

"I mean... I haven't ever felt something like that before..." Jasmine continued, "...and it's not that I don't want it... I really, really do...And I know that no one would ever find out but..."

She realized she wasn't making sense even to herself. She wanted it, and there was no one around who'd ever know... and it felt so very wonderful. She could try it… just this one time, just so she could sleep without this burning feeling. She was too turned on to resist any longer, she needed Rajah to make her cum.

Rajah remained seated near the tub, still looking saddened. Princess Jasmine had made her decision.

Jasmine got up from the edge of the tub, and walked towards Rajah. She got down to the ground, and laid back on her elbows in front of him. Jasmine bit her lip in anticipation, and spread her legs wide. Her perfect pussy absolutely dripping with desire for her tiger's mouth.

"Okay... Just this once Rajah... I want you to make me cum, okay?" Jasmine asked with a smirk, gesturing the tiger to come closer.

Rajah's saddened state immediately vanished, as he quickly skipped over to his master. He stood before her, ready to please her again.

Jasmine ran her hands around her supple breasts and nipples. She worked her way down to her crotch, and put her hands on her upper thighs, then looked up to Rajah. She couldn't stand it. Her heart was racing, and she was

panting already just
from the anticipation of
what was to come.

"Come on, Rajah!" She
said with a pant of lust,
"don't make me wait
anymore!"

Without any more
doubts, Rajah bent down
and began to pleasure his

princess. Her pussy tasted sweet and delicious to the cat, he enjoyed this almost as much as she did. His huge, flat tongue returned to her pussy with a strong, slow lick up her drenched opening.

Jasmine's pussy quivered in pleasure, she let out a high pitched moan and returned to caressing her breasts. Her body was overwhelmed in bliss from this animal tasting her pussy.

"Oh fuck... That's.. incredible... Oh my god..." Jasmine moaned between short, hot breaths.

Rajah stroked Jasmine's pussy lips up and down, his tongue penetrating her whenever he moved to lick her clitoris. Rajah was a quick learner, he could tell was his master wanted from him.

Jasmine's moaning became louder and louder with every stroke of her pussy. Her juices were running down her legs and onto the floor. She shot her head back in pleasure and tensed her back. Jasmine bit her index finger knuckle as Rajah's tongue suddenly struck her clitoris again. She wanted to feel his his tongue deeper inside of her… with her free hand, he pushed the tiger's head deeper into her pussy and thrusted with her hips – Rajah's tongue suddenly slipped deep inside of her, and licked upwards caressing Jasmine's sensitive vaginal walls.

Jasmine screamed in desire, she could feel the pleasure building up and up… She was so close.

Jasmine could've cum on Rajah's first lick, but tried with all her might to resist having an orgasm just yet... she wanted to enjoy every second of her tiger's tongue lapping her burning hot pussy.

"Yes... f-fuck, Rajah.. Yes... Right there!" She blatantly screamed, she couldn't control herself anymore, "Oh my god! Keep going… Oh god, I'm gonna c-cum…make me cum right now Rajah!"

Rajah's tongue wiggled faster and faster in and out of her. He licked up and down her hot pussy and around her clitoris matching the thrusts of

Jasmine's hips. She wrapped her right leg around her tigers neck, pulling him further deeper into her pussy.

"Aah!… Aaah!.. Oh GOD!.. Aahhhh! Rajah! Yes!" Jasmine screamed. Her eyes shut and rolled back. Her hot pussy clenched tight as insane waves of pleasure traveled in her. Rajah's tongue darted in and out, Jasmine couldn't take it anymore.

"Oh GOD! I'm c-cumming Rajah!" she screamed as she thrusted her hips forward and threw her head back. She couldn't breathe, her body was erupting like she'd never felt before.

Jasmine's pussy exploded with passionate, hot juices all over her tiger's tongue as he continued to lick every inch of her, and fill her with insane pleasure.

"Aaaah! Oh my GOD!" Jasmine continued to moan as her orgasm began to shake her entire body. She squeezed her right breast as hard as she could, and pinched her hard nipples. Rajah continued licking his master's clit as she lay back panting with fast, deep breaths with passionate moans between. Her pussy tensed tighter and tighter as her body was completely overwhelmed.

She fell back onto the floor, helplessly limp as her body was engulfed in pleasure. She'd never cum like that in her life, and even so, Rajah continued slowly licking her burning hot pussy. Every stroke felt like she was cumming, all she could think of was wanting to lay there and have Rajah pleasure her all night.

"Oh Rajah..." she said softly, trying to catch her breath, "that was so incredible...I don't know how to repay you..."

The tiger, satisfied in pleasing his master, sat up from between her legs.

Jasmine just lay there for a few moments, taking deep breaths, attempting to regain control of herself. She couldn't believe what she had just done.. She'd let her tiger eat her out – she couldn't believe how wrong it was.. but it was just such an incredible feeling, and easily the most powerful orgasm she'd ever had in her life.

After a few moments spent panting, Jasmine finally gained the strength to sit herself up.. Her hips still shaking, and her pussy still tensed from cumming so hard. Pleasure still coursed throughout her body. She wanted Rajah again, but her womanhood was so sensitive from her amazing orgasm, she'd have to wait until she could handle her pet's amazing tongue again.

She sat up with a huge smile to thank her lovely pet for that service. As soon as her eyes focused upon the large tiger, she notice something different.

"Oh…goodness!" Jasmine said, blushing bright red, as she finally noticed just how aroused Rajah had gotten from this whole experience. Rajah's cock was rock hard, and bounced in anticipation between his legs… He wanted more than to just give pleasure. He wanted Jasmine to return the favor.

Jasmine had never seen Rajah's penis erect before... She was immediately taken aback from how large it was. She was still deeply aroused from his performance, and curious... but knew she couldn't take a cock like Rajah's.

She caught herself with that thought – The only reason she didn't want to let her tiger fuck her senseless is because she didn't think it would fit inside of her? She couldn't believe how she was even considering this…she absolutely couldn't let her tiger fuck her. This was as far as she could go. She wouldn't even consider touching her tigers dick.

"I'm sorry Rajah.. I don't think..." She began, trying to explain, but unable to stop admiring Rajah's large, exquisite cock. She felt the twinge of arousal return to her again.

Rajah let out a small whimper and sat up to all fours – his huge cock bouncing up and down. It was abundantly clear that Rajah's erection wasn't going down any time soon.

"...I mean, I wouldn't even know what to do, Rajah!" Jasmine explained, "I've never even seen a... dick... like that before."

Rajah's eyes were full of excitement, and Jasmine knew that she wanted more pleasure from him. Was she really just making excuses just by saying, 'she wouldn't know what to do?'. Jasmine began to wonder again… Was she really considering pleasuring her tiger? She knew he certainly deserved it, he'd just made her scream and cum like never before. And honestly, Rajah probably knew as much about eating pussy as

Jasmine knows about pleasuring a male… and he did a wonderful job, isn't it only fair to return the favor?

Jasmine couldn't believe her own self – even just thinking about this was turning her on like before. She was growing moist and aroused at just the thought of this. Why was this so exciting for her? And the thought of Rajah fucking her… though Jasmine knew she never could bring herself to do that, she could've probably gotten herself of just by fanaticizing about it. She wanted it so badly.

"Oh my god, Rajah, it's even still getting

bigger..." Jasmine admired as her tiger's cock grew firmer and firmer. Though she'd never seen another male's penis, she knew that Rajah was huge without a doubt. Perhaps, if nothing else, this could be a learning experience for her. Jasmine knew that one day she'd be married to a prince, but without any sexual experience, she'd never know how to please him... Perhaps practicing on Rajah wasn't such a bad idea after all.

Jasmine sat her self up onto her knees, and scooted closer to Rajah. She couldn't look away from his manhood. She never imagined a hard cock this big would be available to her so easily, and with no way for anyone to find out. Truly, this was an opportunity for her… an opportunity she should take advantage of, even if like before, it's just this one time.

"Well..." Jasmine said, "I guess I can try a few things...Don't get your hopes up, I'm just curious what a cock feels like, alright? Not letting you fuck me, Rajah... Like I said, this is just one night of these things happening."

As if Rajah truly understood the words, he

immediately grew excited again.

"Lay down boy," Jasmine said with a sex-driven smirk and a soft giggle, "I wanna see what it's like in my hands"

Rajah followed his instructions, and rolled

over onto his side. His firm cock rested in the air, pointing out, ready for Jasmine.

Jasmine crawled over on all fours, and sat down beside Raja's lower body. Her pussy began to grow wet again as she raised her hand to grasp Raja's huge cock. She bit her lower lip – she was finally going to get to explore a male's erect cock the way she'd always wanted to… this was so exciting and new for her.

She reached forward and wrapped her fingers around the base of Rajah's throbbing cock. The feeling was tense and warm to her…

pleasant even. His cock felt even firmer than it looked.

"Ooh, wow Rajah…" she said, admiring his member, "You're so…hard, boy".

She gave it a slight squeeze, and moved it around a little bit –

playing with it. It was defiantly bigger and harder than any fruit or item she'd ever tried getting herself off with. She wondered if she could make her tiger could cum like she could. Jasmine figured this was the best time to find out how to set off a male.

"So... I guess I go like this?" she rhetorically asked, and started slowly stroking her hand up and down the tigers big dick, "...do you like that, Rajah?"

Rajah gave out a small purr to show that his master was on the right track. She certainly appeared to be eager to learn.

"Hmmm," Jasmine half-said, half-moaned as she began to stroke the tiger's firm cock up and down. She squeezed tightly at the base and worked her way up to the tip, then slowly back up and down.

Her free hand wandered between her legs once again, and began to rub herself as she continued to stroke Rajah's member. Jasmine was so very wet – both from the current situation and from the amazing orgasm she'd just experienced. Yet despite all this, she was still getting more and more turned on as things progressed. She found her self so very excited to make her tiger cum for her.

Jasmine tightened her grip and began stroking Raja's cock faster, occasionally letting out a soft moan as her other hand rubbed circles around her drenched clitoris.

Rajah began to purr softly, and let out small grunts and Jasmine worked his cock up and down.

"You like that, don't you boy?" Jasmine chuckled,

"Your cock is so big...Rajah..."

Jasmine penetrated herself with her middle finger, and began moving it in and out of her while stroking the tiger's dick faster and faster. The small sounds of her slippery fingers sliding in and out matched the rhythm of her strokes on Rajah's dick. Jasmine closed her eyes and began to fantasize that it was Raja's rock hard cock inside of her pussy, sliding in and out, instead of her fingers... She had no idea how firm and hot his cock would be.. the thought of it inside her gave her body shivers with desire.

Jasmine needed to get a better angle to work her tigers member. She wanted to give him the same pleasure he brought her.

"Roll over boy, it'll feel better" she commanded in a soft whisper, "I'll make you cum just like you did for me"

Rajah immediately rolled over into his back, and as quickly as she could, Jasmine climbed atop him and lay her tight naked body across her tiger. She positioned her pussy towards Rajah's head, and straddled him, resting on her knees. Jasmine straightened up, and placed both her hands wrapped around his dick.

She paused for a moment and admired its size once again, and began to think... What else could she do beside just stroking him like this? She could perhaps use her mouth to please him like he had done for her… but this seemed so strange and nasty to Jasmine – was that something women would to to please a man?

As Jasmine became absorbed in her thoughts, she felt a sudden familiar feeling between her legs. Rajah's tongue had found it's way back to

Jasmine's slippery hot pussy, but this time, gave it licks from behind.

"Oh Rajah..." Jasmine moaned as the firm tongue of her tiger traveled up her pussy ... it felt even more amazing from behind, "...that feels incredible"

Jasmine closed her eyes and began to stroke Rajah's cock once again with both her hands. She could put it in her mouth perhaps... but it still seemed like a disgusting act to her... though the thought of doing so did excite her.

Rajah's tongue slipped back inside of Jasmine

and stroked her walls. Jasmine gave a short, quick gasp as chills of pleasure washed over her… she worked his firm cock up and down faster and faster – getting pleasured as she gave it back. She felt as if she could cum again at any point, she was finally working a huge cock like she'd always fantasized and having every inch of her tight, moist pussy licked from behind. She was so turned on, she wanted more...

"F-Fuck it," she said between moans and gasps, ".. I... w-want to suck your cock, Rajah"

She opened her eyes and marveled at the huge member before her. Jasmine licked her lips and bent down towards Rajah's dick. Moments ago she'd swore she wouldn't pleasure her tiger… but now, she was so very aroused, she just wanted his cock in her mouth, and to come with her lovely pet.

Jasmine slowly licked the tip of Rajah's cock, just to give it a taste – Rajah gave out a small purr of delight, and took a moments break from pleasuring Jasmine's womanhood. Jasmine went back down and gave another lick… It tasted like nothing but salty flesh to her, not bad at all. She gave a smile, and moved Rajah's throbbing cock aside her head, and from the base, slowly licked all the way up his dick, circling her lips and tongue around the head. She liked doing this, it was so exciting to her.

"K-keep licking, boy, and I'll make you feel

good, okay?" she said as raised up to the head of his cock again. Rajah immediately returned to lapping Jasmine's soaking wet pussy.

Jasmine bent down and took as much of Rajah's cock into her mouth as she could, getting almost half way down his massive shaft. She began to slowly bob her head up and down, rubbing her tongue around his dick as she did, and letting out muffled moans from the pleasure of Rajah's mouth working her clitoris.

The young princess pumped up and down the base cock with both her hands, and slipped her mouth around his upper shaft and head – grunting with carnal pleasure from both having her mouth fucked by something so large and by being filled with a huge slippery tongue. She absolutely loved the feeling of moving up and down Rajah's dick, just this act almost felt better than getting pleasured herself.

She worked her mouth back and forth faster as she could feel herself growing hotter and closer to climax from Rajah's merciless licking.. Her pussy literally began to throb with desire. She passionately caressed and squeezed her tiger's fat cock up and down the base as she circled her tongue stimulating the tip of Rajah's member. Rajah's tongue felt absolutely divine sliding up and down, in and out of her soaking wet pussy. Jasmine gave long and muffled moans as she could feel herself getting close – she worked Rajah's cock even faster... she couldn't hold off much longer and wanted the tiger to cum with her.

She could hear the deep breaths of Rajah speeding up, her tiger was as close as she was. Jasmine removed her mouth and licked all the way up Rajah's cock, she was so very hungry for the huge cock before her, she wanted it all. Jasmine wasn't thinking anymore, she was purely acting on the impulse of desire.

Jasmine's body twinged and tingled with jolts of ecstasy. Her pussy ready to erupt again. She pumped Rajah's throbbing hard cock as fast as she could manage, and wrapped her mouth around the head of his cock – sucking and licking furiously with moans and pants between... she was so ready to explode.

"C-cum Rajah.. I'm so.. Aaah, I'm so..." Jasmine attempted to say between licks, but being cut off by her own gasps of pleasure, "I-I'm so fucking close Rajah! Cum with me, now! Oh.. oh god pleasee!"

Suddenly Jasmine's back tensed and arched, her hot core finally shooting her past her limits. Her pussy clenched and erupted her hot juices onto the face and tongue of her beautiful tiger. Rajah let out a deep roar as Jasmine whimpered and screamed from the absolute pleasure stemming from her throbbing pussy – yet held up firmly and kept working Rajah's cock.

Rajah had more than he could handle too. As Jasmine's body was overwhelmed and her pussy overflowed with juices and pleasure, Rajah's hard cock was pulsing in Jasmine's hands and mouth – then it suddenly erupted for her. Rajah let out another large roar as his hot cum shot into Jasmine's mouth and lips.

Jasmine hadn't any idea what to do, she couldn't even form thoughts as her body was being rocked and her face was being covered in her tiger's warm seed, but she knew she wanted everything before her. She took her mouth off Rajah's cock as her mouth was filled with his cum – wave's of Rajah's orgasm cause he cock to continue shooting globs onto Jasmine's face and tits. Jasmine licked up and around Rajah's cock as he came, screaming and gasping as she licked up his delicious juices. Rajah's cum ran off her face and down her tits. Jasmine still overwhelmed by her own cumming sat there in ecstasy with her mouth lazily open and load after load of her tiger's cum striking her face.

"OH GOD! Yesss! I want it!" She screamed, as she swallowed what was in her mouth and licked around her lips, "Oh Rajah!"

Rajah's orgasm winded down as small pools of cum still ran down his cock. Jasmine began to regain her ability to see and think as her body began to readjust… she still felt bliss in every part of her body, and continued slowly licking up and down Rajah's cum-covered dick. She had never seen

something like this
before.. she had no idea
it would be so absolutely
wonderful making a
male erupt like that, just
seeing his huge cock
erupt for her as she
sucked it up and down
drove her arousal to a
new level… and the taste..
Jasmine didn't know if
she wanted it because she
was incredibly turned on,

or if she truly just loved her tiger's cock and cum.

Jasmine's pussy, and subsequently the fur beneith it, were soaked with her juices… Rajah's cum ran down her face and supple tits and slowly dripped off of her. Jasmine writhed and moaned in desire as she kept pumping her tigers softening cock. Rajah's panting matched her own.

He was satisfied, but Jasmine still wanted more.. everything she was doing tonight was so new to her.. she never imagined such pleasure being given to her by her own pet. Every new thing she tired felt better than the last – She never wanted it to end.

"Dear lords, Rajah... J-Just fuck me..." she whispered as she continued to stroke his deflating erection with one hand, and fondling her cum-covered breasts with the other... "I want it, I really do... I just want it...inside"

Jasmine still couldn't think straight, she didn't even realize what she was saying – she'd never admit to something so immoral, she had no idea where her control had went.

Rajah began to roll over onto his side, Jasmine

lazily slid off her pet onto the floor soaked with the juices of both their incredible orgasms. Jasmine put herself on all fours, her face down, and ass raised in the air… she subconsciously forced her body into a position for where her tiger could come and fuck her pussy senseless.

"N-no..." she whimpered, arguing with herself..." I- No- I cant do...that..."

She began to regain control of her speech... but what her mouth said her body disagreed with. Her face and body still slick with her tigers cum, and pussy juices running down her legs, she simply had no ability to move.

Rajah began to approach her closer.

"No...Damnit.. I want it.. Rajah, I fucking.. want your cock inside my pussy so bad.. but.. .I just..." she continued to whisper softly between gasps of desire…

Jasmine forced her body to shake, and rolled onto her side. She needed to get away from this situation before she allowed her tiger to fuck her, and she was so very close to letting that happen.

She attempted to stand… but had no feeling in her lower extremities. She rotated, and sat up, facing her lover. Rajah's look was of amazing satisfaction. Jasmine's juices coated the fur around his face and neck, and his own cum still ran down the tip of his flaccid cock.

"Rajah... that was... unbelievable..." she continued, with a sexy smirk of satisfaction. Jasmine could finally begin to feel her sense returning to her, but still remained infatuated with the tiger's cock.

"I've.. never felt anything as intense as that.. I'm still shaking... You're incredible...and..." she continued, "...and you're so big..."

She knew the tiger had no need for praise on his sexual prowess, but just saying the words she was excited her further.

Jasmine knew she was on a slippery slope. If she kept talking like that, she knew soon enough she'd be bent over being pounded by Rajah's huge cock, and she couldn't resist once he started pleasing her – it would be impossible.

"I think..." she said with a sense of disappointment and fortitude, "I think that's enough for tonight boy... I just need to think about..."

Jasmine paused to internally ask herself what she needed to think about... Would she think about actually letting her tiger ravish her like this again? Would he put his cock in her mouth and let him cum all over her body even though she promised this was a one time thing? Would she even... consider letting an animal fuck her?

Jasmine shook her head in confusion... she couldn't answer any of those questions. She just needed to clean herself up, and sleep. She was tiered beyond belief. Cumming twice like that, and having her body completely rocked from the most intense orgasms of her life exhausted her like never before.

Jasmine raised herself to clean off the juices on

her face, and between her legs with one of the soft cloths hanging beside her.

"I can't say this will ever happen like this again… Rajah…" Jasmine said. Rajah tiled his head in inquiry.

"...But, It's been pretty clear I can't say anything for certain now can I?" she joked, "Resisting...the things you can do... was much tougher that I thought..."

She bit her lower lip in attraction as she wiped the cum off of her body with the towel.

"Lets get some sleep, boy" she concluded… Who knew what lay ahead of her… perhaps a good nights sleep could clear her head.

2. Chapter Two: Uncontrollable Rajah

Jasmine yawned begrudgingly as the warm rays of the sun bothered her out of slumber. She gave a deep inhale of the crisp palace air as she rolled among her silk sheets and stretched her lethargic muscles- giving off small groans as she did so.

Her eyes still comfortably shut, she soon realized her usual morning lethargy and crankiness were completely absent- her body was refreshed, she had the wonderful presence of early morning energy, and her mind was relaxed. She'd slept like a baby, and now felt absolutely wonderful… She began to ponder the cause of this unusual early morning bliss.

Jasmine jolted up with a sharp gasp and a fluttering of adrenaline passing through her heart. She sat upright, still unclothed, instinctually covering her naked body with her dark green sheets as she look around the room.

She saw her lovely pet tiger Rajah, still in slumber, curled up on his massive dark red cushion- An item Jasmine had specially made for his bed – in the corner of her chamber.

Her heart began to thump, almost beating out of her chest. Questions began to fill her mind as she started to remember what she had done with that animal the evening prior.

Did last night really happen? Could it have been just a dream? No… she remembered the sensations all too vividly for it to have been a dream.

She began to think back…the memory of Rajah's humongous tiger tongue sliding up and down her quivering womanhood, the moaning and screams she made as he body rocked from pleasure…

even to the point of losing control of her own inhibitions enough to take Rajah's member between her lips- stroking and licking it up and down as Rajah mutually pleased her- until they both finally climaxed together in what was the most intense, body shaking thrill of Jasmine's life.

She placed a hand upon her brow as she began to feel the deep embarrassment in herself for letting something like that happen.

"I just... lost control" she reasoned to herself, taking deep breaths trying to calm her racing mind, "just one night of... experimentation... Just to see what it would feel like...that's all it was... no one could ever find out."

"It sure was quite a rush though," she admitted as she fell back onto her pillows, "I've never been touched quite like that before... "

"...or touched at all, save for myself..." she groaned, twisting her body and unconsciously spreading her legs as she reminisced on Rajah's unbelievable tongue stroking her, and the taste of his throbbing member exploding his warm seed onto her body. She bit her lip and slowly slid her hands up and down her slender thighs… she could feel herself getting excited again.

In a moment of self-realization, she instantly scolded herself and stopped.

"I'm doing it again!" she realized, "This is exactly how it started last time!"

"Started what, Princess? Are you in trouble?" a deep and concerned voice rang from the outside hallway.

Jasmine gave a small jump in surprise to the sudden visitor, but immediately recognized the voice of one of the usual morning guards to which she was quite familiar with.

"No, not at all, Mr. Randesh," she said softly with a small giggle, instantly quelling her inner sexual turmoil and putting on her innocent Princess persona, "I'm perfectly fine.. Just thinking aloud."

"But of course, Princess Jasmine, I understand." the guard continued from outside her room, "May I enter? I have news from your father regarding today's business."

"Just a moment please, I just awoke, and I fear I'm terribly unfit to appear before anyone but my mirror." she replied with all the elegance one would expect from young royalty.

Jasmine quickly hobbled out of bed, her supple naked body radiating in the sunlight. With the cosmetic haste only possessed by a young woman of her age, she clothed herself in her usual green garments and jewelry, and brushed her silky hair into an acceptable form.

Now fit for the public eye, she walked across her chamber to the large gold and red daybed to which she retired to comfortably, conforming herself in an elegant yet relaxed pose- though it was only a guard she would be seeing, she knew she must always remain an item of elegance, class and perfection- it was her primary duty as a princess.

"You may enter now, Mr. Randesh, my apologies for the delay" she spoke softly.

The large wooden door to her room swung open. The muscular and clearly battle torn guard adorned with the standard palace armor and steel halberd walked into her spacious chamber, bowing deeply to the princess upon entrance.

Jasmine gave a nod to signal that he may rise from his bow- as custom by palace etiquette.

"Young Princess Jasmine, if I may," he began, "your father, the Exalted Sultan of Agribah, wishes me to inform you that he is to make an expedition into the next country for diplomatic discussion in regards to furthering trade between our nations. The expedition will require two days travel each way, and many guards to ensure his excellency's safety. Therefore many of the palace officials will be absent in the upcoming days. Your father has instructed a concise unit outside the palace walls- no one will be allowed in or out."

"Very well, then, what does this change for me, though?" she asked

"Nothing Princess, you are to be left to your own accord, your father trusts you- he simply wanted me to inform you that your chamber and the surrounding areas of the palace may seem a bit vacant in the upcoming days."

Jasmine laughed, "As if to say they aren't already!". Though she knew there were hardly any guards to bother her as it was... Having the guarantee of privacy made her 'personal time' a little more accessible without the fear of being walked in on.

"Yes my Princess," the guard said as he bowed, preparing to leave- but quickly stood back up- Rajah had awoken from his sleep and began idly circling around the guard. He was habitually suspicious of anyone besides Jasmine herself.

The guard was visibly uncomfortable by being circled by such a humongous and dangerous animal- even a domesticated one.

"Rajah, come here," she said calmly, the tiger instantly obeying and trotting over to her side. She gave his fur a scruff.

The guard relaxed a bit and began to breathe easier.

"So cautious and intelligent he is... that is truly quite a magnificent creature you have there, Princess." the guard said in praise.

"Oh," Jasmine chuckled, instantly reminded of the 'other' magnificent qualities her animal possessed, "Yes indeed, you truly do not know the half of it." She again chuckled at the inappropriate joke she had made to herself.

The rest of the day progressed uneventfully

to Jasmine, she walked through the palace garden, laid in the sun, and lazily strolled throughout her empty palace. She hadn't paid much attention to Rajah through out the day, she still felt some embarrassment on what she had her tiger do for her- though he was ever-present on her mind.

Later in the afternoon she returned to the palace, and entered the bathing chamber- her mind was still filled with the thoughts of last night, and being that there were no guards to disturb her, she decided to have a bit of fun with herself. Jasmine began to fill the tub with warm water, and sat beside the bathtub on the floor as it filled.

She would still get herself hot simply by the thinking of Rajah's tongue licking her up and down, and though she knew what she did the night prior was absolutely wrong, it had already happened and there was nothing to change that fact- so there would be nothing inherently bad about pleasuring herself to just the memory of it, right? After all, it was just imagination this time.

Keeping her silk top on, she slid her green pants down her legs, and removed them, tossing them aside. She sat with her back resting against the side of the rectangular marble foundation of the tub- the sound of rushing water filling the empty room- and excitedly spread her smooth tanned legs open wide.

Jasmine shut her eyes and began to recall how

just one day prior, she lay in this very room atop her beautiful animal and took almost all of his huge member into her mouth. It was the first cock she had ever tasted, and the first male she had ever fully pleased to climax- and she loved every moment of doing it.

She slid her fingers down her tight little opening which grew slicker the more the fantasized about Rajah's manhood… His throbbing shaft filling her mouth, feeling it's girth in her hands… she even entertained the thought of it fitting inside of her.

Jasmine moaned deeply and slid a finger inside of her, curling it and stroking her sensitive G-Spot with quick motions back and forth… the brief thought of Rajah's cock slipping inside of her almost made her finish instantly. She attempted to insert a second finger into herself- she winced slightly in discomfort as she struggled to fit her middle and ring finger in, but eventually was enjoying the wonderful sensation of having two digits fill her tight little pussy.

Pleasuring herself to the thought of being ravished and fucked by her tiger, Jasmine lost herself in the moment, and did not notice what was standing over her. She felt the warm breath of another being on her face- she instantly opened her eyes in a sudden panic.

It was none other than her tiger again, inches from her face- a devilish

and familiar look in his
eyes.

Jasmine sighed in relief-
thank heavens it wasn't a
guard or a servant that
had walked in on her.
With a short high
pitched moan, she
withdrew her two fingers
from her womanhood,
and placed her arms

around Rajahs neck-scruffing his fur.

"Well hello, I was just thinking about you, Rajah," she said seductively, tapping Rajah on the nose with one her glistening fingers coated in her wetness. Rajah quickly responded by licking at Jasmine's fingers- loving the taste of his master's sex.

Jasmine again giggled, "Don't get any funny ideas, boy, it's not gonna happen."

She moved her left hand to cover her opening with her four fingers, trying to show the eager tiger that she didn't want his attention down there, even though he continued to lick the slick fingers on her right hand.

Rajah scooted himself closer, sitting between comfortably Jasmine's spread legs. She felt a small poke on her hand covering her excited entrance...

Her curiosity and excitement again growing, she leaned to her side to see what had brushed her hand- though she knew what it was, she had spent all day fantasizing about her tiger's member, and couldn't help but want to set her eyes on it again. Jasmine giggled. Rajah was as aroused and excited from the sight of his naked master as ever.

His long tiger cock hovered inches from Jasmine's pussy- only her hand in the way between the two. Upon the sight Rajah's member, Jasmine bit her lip- the object of her fantasy, the cock she had pleased so eagerly the night prior was again ready to be worked by the princess... and was merely inches from entering inside of her body.

Jasmine spoke no words, just took a moment to again fully admire his huge package- what if felt like in her mouth and hands… and what it might feel like slipping in and out her pussy instead of his tongue or her fingers. Lost in her own fantasy, Rajah took advantage of her distraction and pushed his hips forward… the head of his penis gently pushing against her fingers still covering her hot core.

The pressure from Rajah made her four fingers involuntarily spread a bit in the middle- Jasmine's hand now framed her little opening moreso than protected it- allowing Rajah to move his member slightly closer to her. The heat and wetness of her pussy was already coating her fingers completely. Jasmine's growing excitement and imagination overtook her, causing her not fully realize what her tiger's intentions were.

"Oh god... Don't do that..." she whispered in

a hollow plea, as his cock slid past her fingers.

With a slow, deep inhale of a gasp, Jasmine's body was over-washed with chills of pleasure as Rajah's cock brushed against the lips of her pussy- he hadn't entered her, but the sexual bliss of his huge member caressing her slickness caused immeasurable desire.

"R-Rajah..." she whispered... grasping his cock with her free hand, "S-Stop that..."

She began to realize how close he was getting, and scooted her hips back away from her tiger.

Rajah sat back onto his hind legs- his member still within Jasmine's grasp.

Jasmine's breaths were deep and labored, she felt herself returning to her excited state of impulse… Though she had managed to pull her body away from him, even just touching the tiger's member was turning her on, and making her body surge with excitement.

"It's not that I don't want it... I-" she said, trying to find the right excuse and placing her other hand on his cock, idly stroking him up and down with both hands, "It won't even fit inside

Rajah.. There's no way…that… could ever fit inside me."

"And it's wrong…" she continued, not even believing her own words. She'd already done so much with this animal, right and wrong-moral and immoral were almost meaningless words after the events of the night prior.

Even if she wanted to, could she even make it fit? She contemplated this concern staring hungrily upon his thick member- again her curiosity would seem to take control of her. It was probably too long for her to take… and much,

much thicker than the two fingers she just had in her.

"See, I'll prove it to you," she said in a half-hearted attempt to discourage her tiger and herself. Her words were aimed at an excuse she couldn't accommodate the tiger inside her, but in reality Jasmine knew to some degree she wanted to at least try.

She wrapped her legs around Rajah's back and pulled to scoot him closer. Rajah still seated between her thighs eagerly complied. Jasmine lined up the base Rajah's cock between her pussy lips, and rested his thick shaft atop her pelvis- his hard member laying flat on her stomach extending well past her bellybutton.

"That's...Wow...that's how far you'd be inside me, Rajah," She explained, slightly amazed, "I-I can't just take something like that...it's way too big! Besides, I've never had anyone... in me before...". As she spoke Jasmine stroked the tiger's firm member up and down against her tingling body.

Rajah, discouraged, whimpered and slid himself back.

"Don't complain, you're too long! ...And defiantly too thick, boy!" she continued, making excuses not for the tiger, but to discourage herself from trying.

Again Rajah perked up, and hovered his cock outside of Jasmine's wet opening. She grasped him by his shaft in another attempt to demonstrate the problem with his size.

"See?" she asked, placing the head of Rajah's cock at the now soaking wet entrance to her pussy- the tiger's dick brushing against her vaginal lips. Rajah's girth was much to big for her tight little hole, but the tiger wasn't convinced… and truly, neither was Jasmine. She was a virgin to sex, but Rajah was not a human- she long ago surrendered her purity with her devious sexual behavior on her lonesome, and further compounded that fact by allowing her tiger to cum in her mouth and on her body the night prior… With this realization, Jasmine's concerns suddenly switched from the morality aspect of letting her tiger fuck her, to the concern of physically fitting him inside her. She hadn't made up her mind as to if she was ready to try it… perhaps she needed more time to think.

"There's just no way-" she began, quickly cut off from a small advance from Rajah.

"Ahh! Rajaah!" she gasped as the head of the tiger's cock quickly forced its way into her. Jasmine's eyes slammed shut in pain as her entrance began to stretch to accommodate this huge item- It was only the tip of the tiger's cock, but was still bigger than anything she'd ever taken before.

"Ra- Yo- I-" she clumsily stammered, words unable to be formed. Jasmine's eyes fluttered open and closed, her pussy now trembling with unfamiliar mixture of pain and the deep pleasure of being penetrated by her tiger.

She looked down between her legs- it was all happening so fast, did her tiger really just...enter her? She saw her juices running down and around the tiger's cock, only about an inch of his dick was inside her, but she still felt as if she was completely filled up by it. Her mind had no coherent thoughts, her body was racing with desire. Every nerve tingled, every moment almost felt like she was cumming- all branching from the enormous tiger's cock slowly penetrating her.

"Oh my...Oh my, Rajah..." she gasped as the pain diminished and the pleasure continued to rise... she was no longer in control of her own actions, the tiger had overtaken with pleasure. Rajah remained inserted only slightly prodding

Jasmine's little pussy, giving very tiny thrusts as he teased the princess with his cock. Jasmine had her decision made for her, there was absolutely no turning back now- he was inside of her. Her decision to let her tiger do this was either an all or nothing situation- it seemed she was about to experience former.

With her left hand wrapped around the tiger's shaft still guiding it, her right hand began to slowly circle her clitoris. A shock wave of carnal pleasure shot through her again- she was watching her tiger's humongous cock sliding inside of her, and she fucking loved it. Jasmine's mouth remained open ajar, as deep breaths and moans escaped her. Her eyes alternated from fluttering in pleasure and watching her own quivering pussy struggle to take Rajah's dick.

Rajah knew he was pleasing his master, but as always, waited for a sign to continue- if he pushed his cock any further it might hurt the Princess too much.

Jasmine hadn't a moral thought in her brain anymore- Her tiger was going to fuck her, wasn't going to waste time worrying, she was going to just enjoy every single moment of it.

"R-Rajah... " she said between moans, continuing to circle her clitoris and stroke the tiger's shaft.

"S-Stop..." she began...Rajah

immediately discouraged at the notion of stopping,

"S-Stop teasing me… I want more of you… go on boy, put it all the way in…" she meekly whispered with a smirk, "I-I can't fight it anymore… I want your cock in my pussy so bad…F-Fuck me Rajah…"

Rajah's excitement overtook him as he forced his huge dick further inside his Princess. Her slick walls coated the tiger's cock in her juices, making it easer for him to slide in, but it was still much too large for Jasmine.

"Aaah!" Jasmine screamed, pain arising as the tiger's cock stretched her walls pushing forward. The pain, however, was of little consequence as Jasmine began to feel Rajah's cock slip deeper into her- her hot vaginal muscles tightly clenching every inch of his member that was inserted.

"Keep…K-Keep going boy," Jasmine said with one eye closed shut in pain. She slid her body beneath the tiger, laying on her back- her heart racing in excitement and pleasure alike.

Rajah pushed another few inches of himself into

Jasmine, as she raised her hips under him to meet his slow thrust... Jasmine's body twitched...though there was much pain, the thrill and pleasure outweighed it immensely. She didn't know how long she could last even at this rate. Tipping over the edge, all she could focus on mentally was restraining herself from cumming so soon and before she had it all inside her.

"More Rajah! Come on!" she yelled impatiently as she arched her body and aligned her hips with Rajah's member.

The tiger didn't waste a moment being gentle anymore after a command like that. With a swift drive of his hips he pushed the remaining half of his thick cock into Jasmine's pussy with one solid motion.

"Aaaahhh!" Jasmine screamed, slamming her eyes shut and pulling locks of her own hair, trying to displace the pain she felt between her legs, "I-It's too much! Oh my GOD Rajah!"

Her body writhed and twitched in discomfort as her tight virgin pussy tried to stretch to fit this huge member.

"I-I can feel it in m-my belly..." she gasped, her gentle voice quivering. Her breaths were sharp and heavy, chills shot up and down her legs... It was starting to feel pleasurable again.

Jasmine opened her eyes to see if it was finally all in- she started between her arched legs and was truly amazed.

"Oh my…" She said with a gasp, "I-It fit… But, W-wait…I just need… I need a second to adjust boy…"

She could feel her insides struggling to fit this monster, her pussy was clenching his dick so very tightly- she couldn't have taken an inch more, length or girth. It was a perfect fit.

As the pain subsided and the pleasure washed over her body again in ways she couldn't have imagined. The tingles in her legs grew more intense.

She wrapped her arms
around the tigers neck,
and started
determinately into his
eyes,

"Fuck me, Rajah."

Understanding his
master's wishes, Rajah
slowly withdrew himself

from Jasmine, leaving only the tip remaining inserted.

"Aaahhhhhh!" Jasmine groaned, clenching her jaw and closing her eyes. Waves of pleasure from her tiger traveled throughout her body- her back arched and she could feel her vaginal walls clench once again as Rajah exited her. The pleasure was so intense and constant, she couldn't tell if she had just cum, or if this was the constant feeling one had when being fucked by a cock like this-

Without warning Rajah forced his entire member back into Jasmine.

-She learned it was the latter.

Rajah's slow thrusts became rhythmic, Jasmine's attempted to match his motions with her hips. Her high pitched moans filled the room as Rajah slipped his cock in and out of her, slowing building speed. Jasmine could feel her pussy stretch with each stroke, the feeling sent millions of tingles through her body- she almost felt like she was cumming every second, Jasmine couldn't think about anything but the pure bliss of her tiger's humongous dick penetrating her so deeply.

Her screams turned into a low toned moan of pleasure, the pitch traveling up and down with each slam of Rajah's cock. His trusts were becoming harder and firmer for the princess to enjoy. Jasmine lifted her shirt and began to fondle both her breasts and pinch her now erect nipples. Jasmine opened her eyes to watch the tiger's cock coated in her wetness travel in and out.. She loved watching herself be fucked like this. The upward position of Jasmine's hips let Rajah's cock stroke her G-Spot and tickle her clit on each motion, her moans grew louder.

"Oh, Fuck me!... FUCK ME, Rajah!" She screamed as pleasure further overtook her, "Harder boy! I-I want it...HARDER!"

Rajah sped himself up as he pounded Jasmine's young pussy with all the force he could muster.

Rajah loved the sensation of fucking his master, her tight little hole squeezing him so very tightly. The tiger let out a low growl as he began to approach his own edge, fucking Jasmine harder and deeper with each trust. He loved his master, but fucked her like he hated her.

"Oh YESS! I-I L-LOVE IT!" Jasmine screamed, her body twisting in ecstasy, "I love your cock Rajahhh- Y-YES, M-MORE! "

The sound of Jasmine's slick pussy slamming against the base of Rajah's cock made a quick rhythmic wet slapping sound that filled the room-only exceeded by Jasmine's gasps and screams of passion.

Her moaning had turned to screaming as Rajah sped up again and continued to ram his cock down inside her. Her eyes rolled back, her hot pussy throbbed with every motion and thrust. Jasmine's juices dripped off Rajah's shaft and onto the floor. Screaming her tiger's name, Rajah gave a forceful deep thrust of his member that struck the back of Jasmine's pussy- she felt like she was being split in half.

"I C-Can't F-Feel my L-Legs, Rajahh! aaHH!" she screamed.

Jasmine fought with every fiber of her being to last until Rajah could cum with her, but couldn't take the deep pounding pleasure anymore. Jasmine's hips bucked upwards, and her hot little pussy suddenly squeezed even tighter around Rajah's shaft. Her body exploded in primal pleasure as she began to feel this ocean of raw ecstasy overtake her naked body- with a scream, she squeezed both her breasts and threw her hips further up forcing more of Rajah's cock into her. Rajah let out a roar and returned to pounding her pussy harder and faster.

"C-Cum with me Rajahh!" she screamed at the top of her lungs

She could feel every inch of his cock being clenched by her tight walls, yet Rajah unforgivingly continued to fuck her faster and faster. Jasmine could feel her climax begin explode through out her body, but she held on for her tiger even as her entire body became numb. Rajah let another roar escape, he continued to thrust deeply into her as his cock finally erupted his hot thick load shooting inside and filling Jasmine's pussy completely-his strokes continued as his cum spilled out of his master, landing upon Jasmine's legs and body.

Another scream escaped Jasmine's lips from the feeling of her tiger's hot cum shooting inside her-it set her absolutely over the edge, cumming unimaginably harder than she ever dreamed. Her quivering pussy erupted with juices around Rajah's throbbing dick, her trembling legs shook vigorously as her orgasm resonated through her entire body. Her numb body was suddenly overtaken by the explosive frenzy of sexual pleasure. She tossed her head back and forth, cumming like this was too much to handle. Her screaming became louder as her and her tiger rode their waves of ecstasy together- she'd never experienced a pleasure this long- it grew more intense with every moment that hot tiger cock stay thrusted deep inside her and spilled its cum.

Her and her tiger's juices dripped to the floor, she moaned Rajah's name over and over as her body finally collapsed under the him, his cock still fully inserted. Jasmine panted like an animal in heat and continued to run her hands up and down her body as the pleasure traveled back and forth, slowly subsiding, but never vanishing.

After a moment, Rajah finally withdrew himself completely from his master- his cock coated in her warm wetness and his own cum. Jasmine gave a high pitched whimper as he unexpectedly pulled himself out. She was drunk with pleasure.

"I, y'ou, the-ca'tr" Jasmine struggled to speak, her body still quivering in bliss, she could barely form any words at all.

"Y-you were
incredible... Rajahh"
she finally managed to
say, her tone heavy with
her now unhindered
sexual desire. She put
her hands around the
tiger, and pulled herself
up to a seated position,
"I can't b-believe that
was w-what I was
missing. I can't believe

how wonderful you can make me feel- what you can do to my body- how b-big and hard you are- how you can fuck me."

She couldn't believe the way she was talking, but loved praising her tiger- she no longer had any shame about her mutual sexual desire with her animal. This colossally outclassed anything she could do to her body on her own. Now that she had already made the decision, and been fucked by her tiger, she could do it as often and as much as she pleased with no inner turmoil.

Jasmine quickly flipped her body over, struggling with her legs still not regaining all feeling from her body rocking orgasm. She removed her top completely, and tossed it across the room, then settled on her hands and knees- her slender, sexy legs poisoned far apart in a very inviting manner to Rajah.

She looked back at her tiger over her shoulder,

slinging her messy hair across her naked back.

"Well," she said with the most seductive and devilish of grins, "We're not done, what are you waiting for?"

Jasmine prepared again to have her body fucked senseless by her animal-she wanted to try everything… she didn't care where, or how, she just wanted her tiger's cock in her… And after a performance like that, she intended to let Rajah do whatever he wanted with her body.

The End